THIS BLOOMSBURY BOOK

BELONGS TO

....................................

For Jamie-Lee, Tom & Ash, & Alex,
with love
D.C.

To little beasties everywhere
K.H.-J.

Bloomsbury Publishing, London, New Delhi, New York and Sydney

First published in Great Britain in April 2011 by Bloomsbury Publishing Plc
50 Bedford Square, London, WC1B 3DP



A CIP catalogue record of this book is available from the British Library

ISBN 978 1 4088 0002 7

Printed in China by LEO Paper Product Ltd, HeShan

3 5 7 9 10 8 6 4

All papers used by Bloomsbury Publishing are natural, recyclable products made
from wood grown in well-managed forests. The manufacturing processes
conform to the environmental regulations of the country of origin

www.bloomsbury.com

# Don't Wake the Beastie!

Dawn Casey

Illustrated by Kirsteen Harris-Jones

BLOOMSBURY

LONDON NEW DELHI NEW YORK SYDNEY

SNNNOR

Under the tree, the Beastie slept.

E . . .

'SNOINK! SNOINK!' said Pig. 'Yummy honey!'

'Shhh,' said Donkey. 'Don't wake the Beastie! He loves eating piggies and he'll snap you up.'

'Well, *I* love eating honey,' said Pig. 'Help me, pleeease!'

'Oh, all right,' said Donkey, 'but be QUIET.'

Donkey winced as Pig huffed up on to his back, but he didn't say a word.

On the tips
of his trotters,

Pig **stretched** towards the honey . . .

'It's no good,' said Pig.
'I can't reach.'

Under the tree, the Beastie yawned
and stretched his razor-claws and . . .

...SN

'Shhh,' said Donkey and Pig. 'Don't wake the Beastie!'

'He loves eating little lambies,' said Pig. 'He'll crunch and munch you all up.'

'Just because I'm little, I'm not scared,' bleated Lamb.

Lamb sprang on to Pig's back. Pig flinched as Lamb squished his ear, but he didn't make a sound.

Lamb **stretched** towards the honey . . .

'I can't reach.'

Under the tree, the Beastie
grimaced and grunted
and growled and . . .

. . . SNNNORE!

'RUFF! RUFF!'

'Shhh,' said Donkey
and Pig and Lamb.
'Don't wake the Beastie!'

'He loves eating dogs,'
said Lamb. 'He'll
slobber you up
and slurp
you down.'

'I love helping,'
said Dog, bounding
around in excitement.
Up Dog scrambled,
over Donkey's rear,
up Pig's tail, across
Lamb's fleece, right to
the top of Lamb's head.

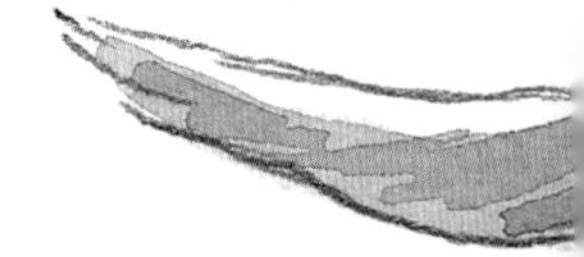

Dog was heavy. Lamb closed her eyes tight. Donkey stuck out his tongue, but he didn't make a sound.

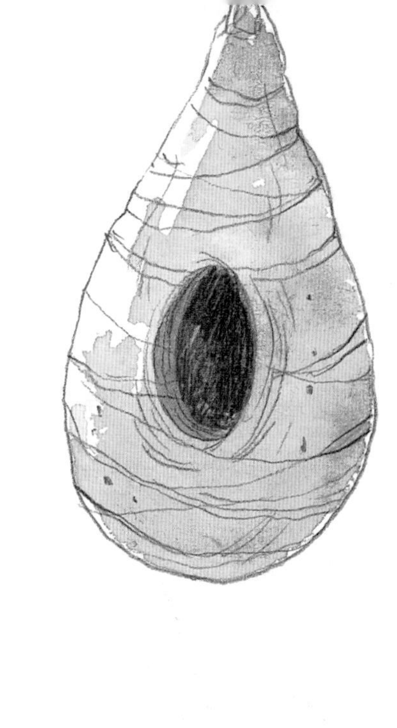

Dog **stretched** towards the honey . . .

'I can't reach.'

Under the tree, the Beastie flicked out his sticky tongue and licked up a fly and . . .

'COCK-A-DOODLE-DOO!'

'Shhh,' hissed Donkey and Pig and Lamb and Dog. 'Don't wake the Beastie!'

'He'll gobble you up for sure,' said Dog.

Cockerel puffed up his feathers. 'I can be as quiet as anyone.' And he hopped on to Dog's head.

'Be careful,' said Dog. 'Your feathers tickle.'

'Dog!' hissed all the animals. 'Shhh!'

Under the tree, the Beastie
flared his hairy nostrils
and snorted smoke and . . .

# . . .SNNNORE!

Quietly, quietly,
the animals reached up.

Cockerel wobbled.

He balanced.

He **stretched** towards the honey . . .

'I've got it!' he crowed.

Under the tree,
the Beastie rolled
over and . . .

'BZ

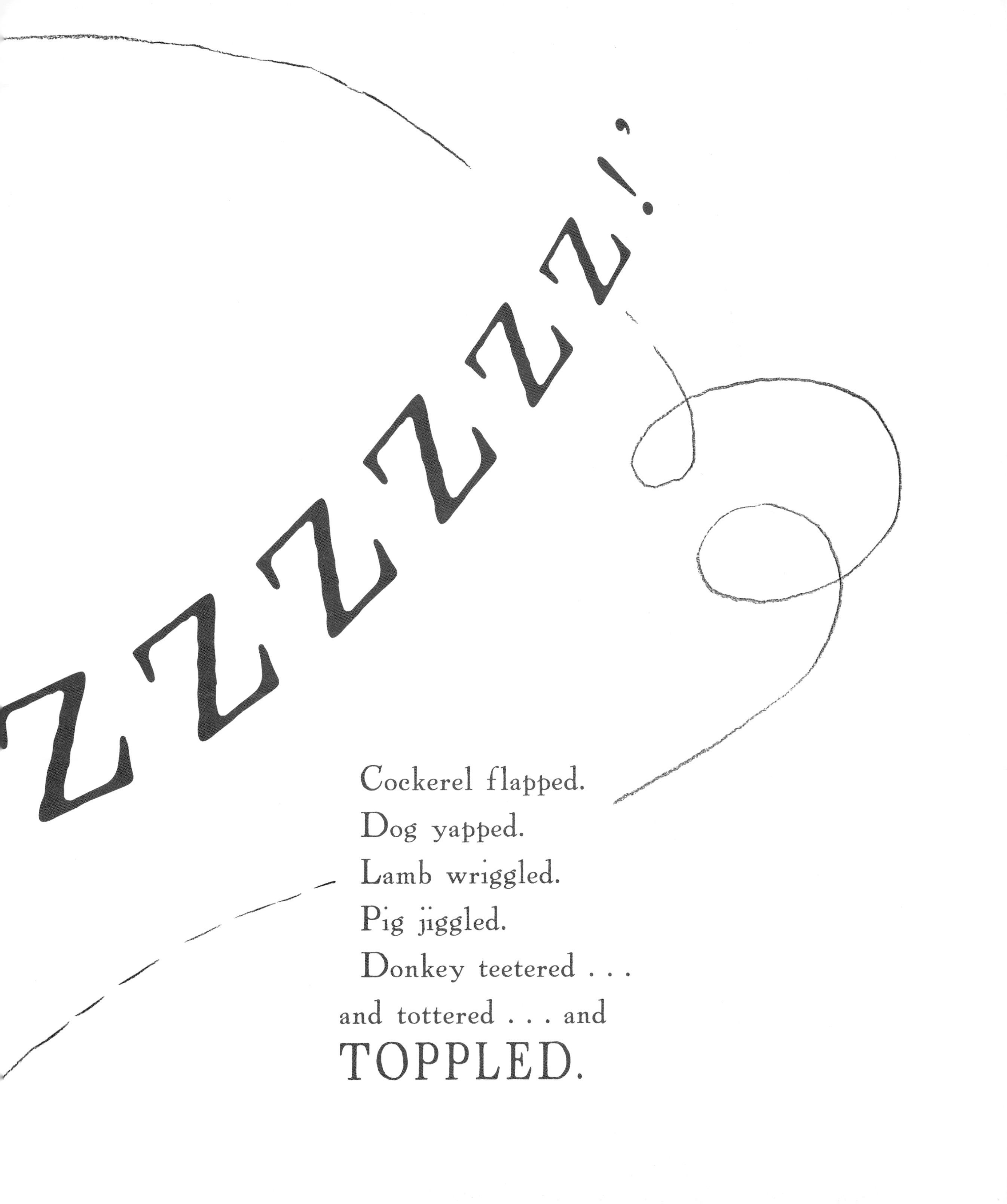


Cockerel flapped.
Dog yapped.
Lamb wriggled.
Pig jiggled.
Donkey teetered . . .
and tottered . . . and
TOPPLED.

Down came Cockerel.
'COCK-A-DOODLE-DOO!'
Down came Dog.
'RUFF!'
Down came Lamb.
'BAAAAA!'
Down came Pig.
'SNOINK!'

Down came Donkey.
'EEEE-OOR!'
And down came the honeycomb.
BUMP!
BUMP!
BUMP!

Under the tree, the Beastie was **not** asleep now! He flexed his claws and opened his jaws. The Beastie looked from Donkey to Pig, from Lamb to Dog to Cockerel. He licked his razor-teeth.

'ROAR! Now for some snapping, now for some crunching, now for some slurping and gobbling and munching . . .

I spy my favourite food . . .

. . . Honey!'

## Enjoy these grrreat animal tales from Bloomsbury Children's Books . . .

*Ribbit Rabbit*

by Candace Ryan
& illustrated by Mike Lowery

*More, More, More!*

by Dawn Casey
& illustrated by Nick Price

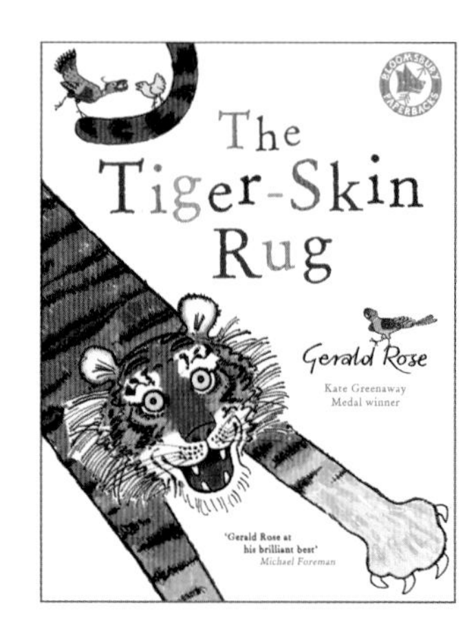


*The Tiger-Skin Rug*

by Gerald Rose

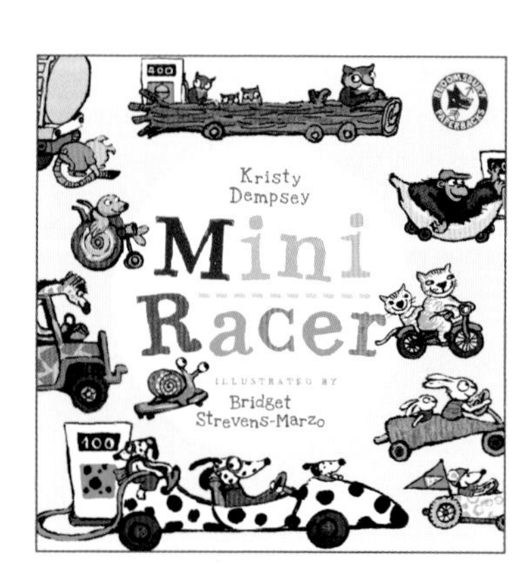


*Mini Racer*

by Kristy Dempsey
& illustrated by Bridget Strevens-Marzo